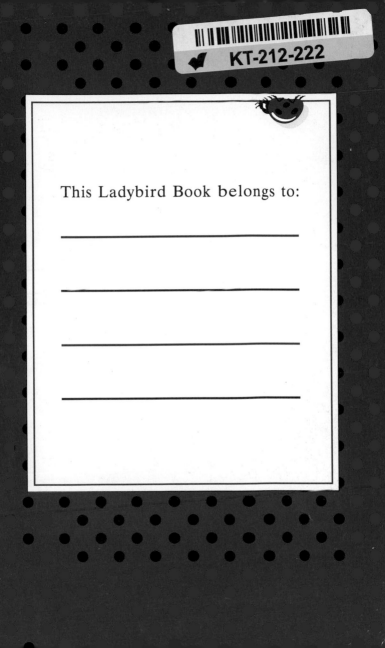

This Ladybird Book belongs to:

_____

_____

_____

_____

All children
have a great ambition …
to read by themselves.

Through traditional and popular stories, each title
in the **Read It Yourself** series introduces children to
the most commonly used words in the English
language (*Key Words*), plus additional words
necessary to tell the story.
The additional words appearing in this book are
listed below.

turnip, seeds, plants, grow,
enormous, dinner, mouse, carry

Ladybird books are widely available, but in case of
difficulty may be ordered by post or telephone from:

Ladybird Books – Cash Sales Department
Littlegate Road Paignton Devon TQ3 3BE
Telephone 0803 554761

A catalogue record for this book is available
from the British Library

Published by Ladybird Books Ltd Loughborough Leicestershire UK
Ladybird Books Inc Auburn Maine 04210 USA

The Enormous Turnip

adapted by Fran Hunia
from the traditional tale
illustrated by John Dyke

The old man has
some turnip seeds.
He plants
the seeds.

He waters the seeds.
The turnip seeds grow.

One turnip grows
and
grows
and
grows!

It is
enormous!

The old man says,
I want some turnip
for dinner.

He pulls and pulls,
but he can't pull up
the enormous turnip.

The old man calls
to the old woman.
Come and help me
to pull up
this turnip,
he says.

It is **enormous**.

The old woman pulls
the old man
and the old man pulls
the turnip.

They pull and pull,
but they can't pull up
the enormous turnip.

The old woman calls
to a boy.
Come and help us
to pull up
this enormous turnip,
she says.

The boy pulls
the old woman
and the old woman
pulls the old man
and the old man
pulls the turnip.
They pull and pull,
but they can't
pull up
the enormous turnip.

The boy calls
to a girl.
Come and help us
to pull up
this enormous turnip,
he says.

The girl pulls the boy
and the boy pulls
the old woman
and the old woman
pulls the old man
and the old man
pulls the turnip.

They pull and pull,
but they can't pull up
the enormous turnip.

The girl calls
to a dog.
Come and help us
to pull up
this enormous turnip,
she says.

The dog pulls
the girl
and the girl pulls
the boy
and the boy pulls
the old woman
and the old woman
pulls the old man
and the old man
pulls the turnip.

They pull and pull,
but they can't pull up
the enormous turnip.

The dog calls
to a cat.
Come and help us
to pull up
this enormous turnip,
he says.

The cat pulls
the dog
and the dog
pulls the girl
and the girl
pulls the boy
and the boy pulls
the old woman

and the old woman
pulls the old man
and the old man
pulls the turnip.
They pull and pull,
but they can't pull up
the enormous turnip.

The cat calls
to a mouse.

Come and help us
to pull up
this enormous turnip,
she says.

The mouse pulls
the cat
and the cat pulls
the dog
and the dog pulls
the girl
and the girl pulls
the boy

and the boy pulls
the old woman
and the old woman
pulls the old man
and the old man
pulls the turnip.

They pull and pull
and . . .

up comes the enormous turnip!

They all help
to carry the turnip
home.

And they all have turnip for dinner.